THE
SERPENT'S
SHADOW

THE GRAPHIC NOVEL

RICK RIORDAN

Adapted and Illustrated by
ORPHEUS COLLAR

Lettered by
CHRIS DICKEY

Colour Assists by
STEPHANIE   **ALADDIN**   **CAM**
BROWN   **COLLAR**   **FLOYD**

DALLAS, TEXAS.
DALLAS ART MUSEUM.
11:30 P.M.

KING TUT

KING TUT

DALLAS MUSEUM OF ART

It seemed incredible that not even a year had passed since my *brother Carter* and I learned we were *blood of the pharaohs*, imbued with the gift of Egyptian magic, completely clueless of our heritage and powers.

If you told us that nine months later we'd be hobnobbing with high society from the Dallas chapter of the *House of Life*, I would have laughed!

Unfortunately, our reason for visiting was not to party.

THIS IS A DAPPER GROUP! SHAME WE'RE WEARING *COMBAT GEAR* FOR A *GALA*.

WE HAVE TO BE PREPARED FOR ANYTHING TONIGHT. LOOK, THERE'S OUR MAN.

CHAPTER 1

SO, ARE YOU HERE WITH A PLAN TO STOP APOPHIS'S RISE?

A PLAN INVOLVING *THE GODS*?

Six months ago, our "Plan A" to overcome Apophis was to revive his archenemy, the sun god Ra.

We succeeded, but Ra had woken up senile, demented, and completely helpless.

Our best allies, the gods of Egypt, were now too distracted babysitting the sun god to give us much help.

Six months later, the only Plan B we'd come up with was too horrible to contemplate.

THE GODS ARE BUSY.

WE'RE WORKING ON A PLAN OF ATTACK. BUT TONIGHT WE'RE HERE ON DEFENSE.

KING TUT

KING TUT

DALLAS MUSEUM OF A[

DEFENSE.

YOU THINK YOU CAN PROTECT DALLAS BETTER THAN OUR MAGICIANS? I HOPE YOUR TEAM IS TOP-NOTCH.

THEY'RE *AMAZING!* COME ON, WE'LL INTRODUCE YOU.

Our crack squad of magicians was busy raiding the gift shop.

THIS IS YOUR AMAZING TEAM?

YES. THESE ARE SOME OF OUR BEST INITIATES!

WALT IS OUR RESIDENT MASTER OF AMULETS AND CHARMS.

ALYSSA FOLLOWS THE PATH OF **GEB**, THE EARTH GOD.

KHUFU IS OUR BABOON.

AAGH!

AND FELIX...

I FOUND MY PATH. I'M SUPPOSED TO FOLLOW THE **GOD OF ICE!**

EGYPT IS A DESERT. WHO'S THE ICE GOD?

I HAVE NO IDEA!

DON'T WORRY ABOUT THE GIFT SHOP. WE'LL CLEAN IT UP, MR. GRISSOM! BUT FIRST, CAN YOU SHOW US YOUR EGYPTIAN COLLECTION?

The entrance to Dallas's Egyptian wing was flanked by two sphinxes with the bodies of lions and the heads of rams.

THESE *CRIOSPHINXES* WERE THE ONLY GUARDIANS MOST PHARAOHS NEEDED TO KEEP THEIR TEMPLES SAFE.

IF ONLY IT WERE STILL THAT SIMPLE.

IF YOU FIND ANY WEAKNESS IN OUR DEFENSES, LET ME KNOW. I'M GOING TO GO BACK TO ENTERTAINING MY GUESTS!

YES, SIR!

We fanned out into the Egyptian wing, inspecting artifacts for signs of Apophis.

Egyptian exhibits always brought up bad memories... gods I'd met and fought in person, reminders of the *afterlife*.

Most upsetting of all: a small alabaster statue of our friend *Bes, the dwarf god.*

We'd only known Bes for a few days, but he'd literally sacrificed his soul to help us.

Now each time I saw him I was reminded of a debt I could never repay.

IT'S OKAY, SADIE. YOU CAN'T SAVE *EVERYBODY.*

Walt was one to talk. He suffered from an eons-old, incurable curse on his bloodline.

It got worse every time he used his own magic, so he only drew power from amulets.

WHAT IS IT, KHUFU? DO YOU SMELL DANGER?

AAGH!

Khufu pointed to a trail of destruction racing toward us.

It missed Carter, and came straight at Walt and me!

I grabbed my wand...

...and spoke the first command word that came to mind.

DROWAH!*

*"Boundary!"

HUMAN CIVILIZATION HASSS GROWN OLD AND ROTTEN.

WITH EVERY ATTACK, CHAOSSS INCREASESSS.

SOON, IT WILL BE ENOUGH FOR ME TO RISSSSE.

I WILL SSSWALLOW THE SUN GOD AND PLUNGE THE WORLD INTO DARKNESSSS!

At the entrance to the room, the two obsidian criosphinxes turned and blocked the exit.

I THINK I'LL DESTROY YOU WITH THE GUARDIANS OF MA'AT.

YES, THAT WILL BE AMUSING.

Fire-breathing sheep. Oh joy.

INITIATES, THIS IS WHAT WE'VE TRAINED FOR.

LIKE WE'VE PRACTICED. THREE...TWO... ONE...

The room was filled with the writhing coils of a giant red snake. The magic of Apophis encircled my friends, pulling apart the museum from foundation to ceiling.

It was now or never: I had to restore order before the building toppled on us.

I channeled the power of the **goddess Isis**. I forced myself to focus, and I spoke the most powerful of all divine words:

MA'AT!

AGH?

WH-WHAT HAPPENED? HOW LONG...?

YOU WERE DEAD FOR TWO MINUTES, SADIE.

I MEAN, NO HEARTBEAT.

WE WERE AFRAID...

I glanced around to see the room hadn't collapsed. But the entire exhibit was in ruins.

I HAVE A FEELING WE WON'T BE INVITED BACK AS "FRIENDS OF THE DALLAS MUSEUM" ANYTIME SOON.

YOU GUYS DID GREAT!

LET'S CHECK ON JD GRISSOM AND THE DALLAS MAGICIANS.

The first time my brother and I entered an Egyptian museum together, we lost our father.

The second time, we unleashed some demons and almost lost an initiate.

No casualties this time, except me--so far.

I'd love to say we found all the Texas magicians safe and sound. We didn't.

The well-kept lawn that had been host to a thriving party was now a crater as big as an Olympic pool.

I wondered how many magicians had died.

JD GRISSOM. THE TEXANS--

THEY'RE *DEAD*.

ALL OF THEM.

We didn't have time to mourn our comrades. The mortal authorities would be arriving soon to check out the scene.

FWEET

Our ride home glided over from the museum's roof.

Freak the griffin is a beautiful monster, if you like psychotic falcon-headed lions.

TAKE US **HOME**, BUDDY.

FREEAK!

Tears stung my eyes, and it wasn't from the wind.

Toronto.

Chicago.

Mexico City.

And now... *Dallas.*

Fog swallowed the boat. With a defiant squawk, Freak pulled us into the **Duat.**

FREE... ...AK!

The Duat's fog cleared as we sailed over New York's East River toward home.

Regular mortals wouldn't see anything but a huge dilapidated warehouse, but to magicians, **Brooklyn House** was as obvious as a lighthouse!

It was almost midnight, but the **Great Room** was still buzzing with activity.

Our youngest initiates, **the ankle-biters**, drew crayon pictures on the floor.

FREEAK!

The rest watched the news. The Dallas disaster was all over it.

BREAKING NEWS
DESTRUCTION IN DALLAS
FREAK GAS PIPE EXPLOSION CAUSE
S&P   55.32   STAY CURRENT WITH LATE BREAKIN

Living at Brooklyn House felt like having a dozen brothers and sisters. It helped during times of grief.

We walked to the most secure room in the house: the library. It's where we hatched all our most secret and dangerous plans, and where we held our most powerful artifact.

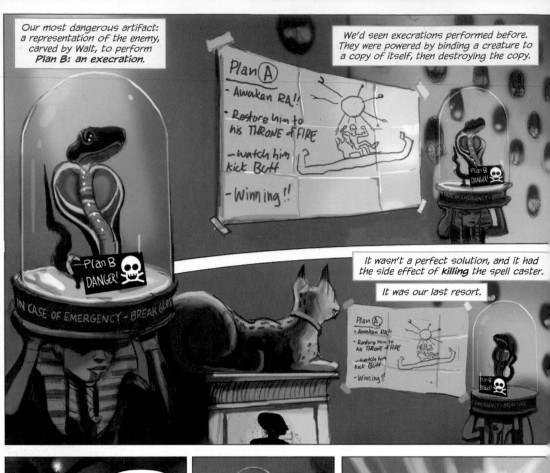

Our most dangerous artifact: a representation of the enemy, carved by Walt, to perform **Plan B**: an execration.

We'd seen execrations performed before. They were powered by binding a creature to a copy of itself, then destroying the copy.

It wasn't a perfect solution, and it had the side effect of **killing** the spell caster.

It was our last resort.

MUFFIN? HOW DID YOU GET DOWN HERE?

MROORW!

BAST! AREN'T YOU SUPPOSED TO BE AT YOUR, UM...*NIGHT JOB?*

BABYSITTING *RA?* YES, I LEFT MY POST.

WE FELT A *RIPPLE IN THE DUAT,* A DEEP DISTURBANCE.

I HAD TO MAKE SURE MY KITTENS WERE ALIVE.

APOPHIS IS *RISING.* WE COULDN'T STOP HIM FROM KILLING ALL OF DALLAS.

THE ATTACKS ARE GETTING *WORSE.*

Bast pointed to a curious little box.

I KNOW YOU ARE CONTEMPLATING AN *EXECRATION.* SO WE GODS HAVE FOUND A WAY TO POWER THE SPELL WITHOUT SACRIFICING YOUR OWN LIVES.

IT'S *EMPTY.*

LOOK *CLOSER.*

I peered through the Duat... to see a little shadow.

PHARAOHS OFTEN BURIED THEIR *SHADOWS* WITHIN A PROTECTIVE SHADOW BOX LIKE THIS SO IT WOULD NOT BE LOST IN THE AFTERLIFE.

IT WAS MORE THAN A TRICK OF THE LIGHT-- IT WAS A PART OF THEIR *SOUL.*

THEN THERE'S THE *IB, THE HEART.*

THE RECORD OF GOOD AND BAD DEEDS, IT'S THE BIT THEY WEIGH ON THE SCALES OF JUSTICE IN THE AFTERLIFE.

Dead souls' hearts are weighed on the scales of justice against the feather of truth. If they come up wicked or untruthful, their hearts are eaten by the devourer of souls, Ammit. Or as I called him, "Poochiekins."

LAST IS THE *SHEUT, THE SHADOW OF THE SOUL.*

MORE THAN A PHYSICAL SHADOW, THE SHEUT IS THE SILHOUETTE OF THE SOUL. IT CONTAINS A COPY OF ITS NEEDS AND DESIRES.

IN ANCIENT TIMES, THE EGYPTIANS USED THE *SAME WORD* FOR STATUE AND SHADOW, BECAUSE THEY'RE BOTH SMALLER COPIES OF AN OBJECT. THEY WERE *BOTH* CALLED A SHEUT.

SHADOWS AS COPIES...

WITH A *STANDARD EXECRATION*, YOU DESTROY A STATUE THAT REPRESENTS THE ENEMY. BUT IF THE SPELL COULD BE CRANKED UP BY DESTROYING A MORE POWERFUL REPRESENTATION...

GET SOME REST. ANSWERS MAY COME EASIER IN THE DAYLIGHT.

I GUESS THE QUESTION REMAINS IF APOPHIS HAS A SHADOW AND WHERE WE CAN FIND IT.

YAAWN

Sleep: easier said than done. And not just because I had a snoring baboon for a roommate.

YOU'RE STILL PONDERING AN EXECRATION?

I STILL THINK A FRONTAL ASSAULT IS THE WAY TO GO.

HORUS?

YOU'RE LOOKING VERY, UH...

...VERY PIGEONLY.

I LOOKED FOR A *FALCON*, BUT THEY'RE A LITTLE SCARCE IN *NEW YORK*.

I WANTED SOMETHING WITH WINGS. PIGEONS HAVE ADAPTED WELL TO CITIES AND AREN'T SCARED OF PEOPLE.

NOBLE BIRDS, DON'T YOU THINK?

NOBLE. YEAH, THAT'S THE FIRST WORD THAT COMES TO MIND WHEN I THINK OF PIGEONS.

LET IT BE KNOWN THAT YOU ARE STILL MY FAVORITE *HOST*.

WE ARE STRONG ENOUGH, YOU AND I. WE SHOULD COMBINE FORCES, CARTER. LET ME SHARE YOUR FORM AS I ONCE DID. WE COULD LEAD THE ARMIES OF GODS AND MEN AND DEFEAT THE SERPENT.

TOGETHER, WE'LL RULE THE WORLD.

I'M NOT WORRIED ABOUT RULING THE WORLD. WE NEED TO SAVE IT!

DO YOU KNOW ANYTHING ABOUT APOPHIS'S SHEUT?

ALL LIVING BEINGS HAVE A SHEUT. EVEN GODS. EVEN APOPHIS.

AS FOR FINDING IT... YOU ASK A GOD OF WAR ABOUT A SUBJECT BEST SUITED FOR A GOD OF KNOWLEDGE.

THOTH IS STILL IN TENNESSEE AT THAT RIDICULOUS PYRAMID OF HIS. CONSULT WITH HIM.

AND BEFORE YOU GO, SUIT UP. IT COULD BE DANGEROUS.

LOSING CONTROL OF HOST--

--WE'LL TALK LATER.

COO.

PLOP

The next day, I passed under the giant statue of Thoth in the Great Room. It was time to go to Memphis.

News had traveled quickly around the world about Dallas within the magician community. But if the apocalypse was happening, you couldn't tell by our initiates.

Considering how badly last night had turned out, everyone seemed in strangely good spirits.

ANYBODY SEEN SADIE?

SHE'S IN HER ROOM!

CHAPTER 2

KNOCK KNOCK

HULLO, BROTHER DEAREST. COME TO GET TIPS FOR WHAT TO WEAR TO THE DANCE?

WHAT? NO, UH-- DANCE?

BROOKLYN ACADEMY FOR THE GIFTED HAS INVITED US TO ITS FIRST DANCE TONIGHT! I'VE MENTIONED IT TO YOU A DOZEN TIMES. THREE OTHER SCHOOLS WILL BE THERE.

THE TIMING COULDN'T BE BETTER. WE NEED SOMETHING TO BOOST OUR SPIRITS AFTER DALLAS. ANYWAY, WHAT DO YOU WANT?

HORUS VISITED ME LAST NIGHT. HE SAYS THOTH MAY KNOW HOW TO FIND AND CAPTURE APOPHIS'S SHADOW.

YES, LET'S GO! AFTER THE DANCE.

THOTH MAY BE UNDER ATTACK.

WE CAN'T WAIT.

NOT EVEN FOR A FEW EXTRA HOURS? OKAY THEN, YOU VISIT THOTH.

YOU'RE KIDDING!

I'M THINKING ABOUT PLANS FOR DOOMSDAY, AND YOU'RE WORRIED ABOUT BEING LATE TO A DANCE?

TAKE AN INITIATE WHO DOESN'T CARE ABOUT THE DANCE. I'LL MAKE SURE OUR TROOPS ARE WELL RESTED AND ENTERTAINED BEFORE THE BIG BATTLE BEGINS.

EVEN ARMIES IN THE FIELD FIGHT BETTER WHEN THEY TAKE BREAKS FOR ENTERTAINMENT, CARTER!

I'M SURE SOME GENERAL SOMEWHERE HAS SAID THAT.

GRRRR.

Of *course* we had serious business to deal with. That's why I insisted on partying first.

I chose black lowlights, a strapless dress, and dark makeup for that fresh risen-from-the-grave look.

For jewelry, I wore a pendant Walt had given me with the Egyptian symbol of eternity, *shen*.

Walt had a matching amulet. Unfortunately, the shen amulets didn't mean we were dating exclusively.

Or even dating at all.

The only other boy I liked, **Anubis**, was a *god* who never visited. If Walt had asked me out, I think I would've been fine with it.

But Walt was *dying*. He had this silly idea that it would be unfair to me if we started a relationship under those circumstances.

We were stuck in a **maddening limbo**-- flirting, talking for hours, but eventually Walt would always pull away and shut me out.

By **sunset**, I was ready to lead my troops into battle.

I marched straight to the Great Room...

...where I saw something that made my blood curdle.

WALT STONE!

?

WHAT ARE YOU DOING IN COMBAT GEAR?

WE HAVE A DANCE TO GO TO!!

I'M GOING WITH CARTER TO SEEK ANSWERS FROM THOTH IN MEMPHIS. SHADOW MAGIC MAY BE OUR BEST HOPE TO BEAT APOPHIS!

BUT WHAT ABOUT YOUR *CURSE*?! YOU'RE SAFER GOING TO THE DANCE, WALT.

THERE'S LESS CHANCE YOU'LL HAVE TO USE MAGIC TO DEFEND YOURSELF.

I'M BRINGING MY BEST DEFENSIVE TALISMANS IN CASE WE RUN INTO TROUBLE.

IF THINGS GET TOO CRAZY IN MEMPHIS, I CAN CONTACT YOU THROUGH MY *SHEN AMULET*.

Our shen amulets provided us a magic line of communication. In emergencies, they even gave us the ability to summon the other person to our side.

AND I CAN ALREADY FEEL THROUGH THE SHEN AMULET THAT I CAN'T CONVINCE YOU TO COME WITH US.

WALT--

--IF I DON'T GO, THE OTHERS MIGHT FEEL OBLIGED TO STAY TOO.

AFTER DALLAS, WE NEED A GOOD NIGHT!

Walt flew off with Carter, taking all the joy out of the evening for me.

I'd still have to go and pretend to have fun.

I wondered if this was what being a grown-up felt like.

BROOKLYN ACADEMY FOR THE GIFTED (BAG ACADEMY).

GRAB YOUR DATE, THIS ONE'S GOING TO BE A SLOOOW DANCE.

Brooklyn Academy for the Gifted Fall Formal

Great, a slow dance.

Look at all the happy people dancing with their dates. Joy.

HELLO, SADIE.

MAY I HAVE THIS DANCE?

I gazed up at *Anubis's* warm eyes and his exquisite lips-- the *first* I'd ever kissed.

ANUBIS?!

It happened on my birthday last spring, and though I thought I'd gotten over it, his presence now made all the old feelings come back.

Push it aside, Sadie.

I THOUGHT YOU COULD ONLY APPEAR IN PLACES OF DEATH.

THIS *IS* A PLACE OF DEATH, SADIE.

Suddenly, spirits were twirling all around us, luminous apparitions in eighteenth-century clothes: the red uniforms of British regulars and ragtag militia outfits.

They pirouetted with lady ghosts in plain farm dresses or fancy silk.

THE *BATTLE OF BROOKLYN HEIGHTS,* 1776.

HUNDREDS OF AMERICAN AND BRITISH TROOPS DIED RIGHT WHERE WE'RE DANCING.

The ghosts seemed to be dancing to a different song.

I strained my ears and could faintly hear violins and a cello.

HOW *ROMANTIC*. YOU CERTAINLY KNOW HOW TO SHOW A GIRL A GOOD TIME.

IT'S A *LOOPHOLE*, I ADMIT.

THESE GHOSTS COULD USE A NIGHT OF ENTERTAINMENT, JUST LIKE YOUR INITIATES.

BUT TO THE PURPOSE OF MY VISIT...

THERE'S BEEN GRUMBLING AMONG THE GODS ABOUT OUR *SITUATION*.

I'VE COME TO SAY *GOOD-BYE*, SADIE.

"OUR SITUATION"?

US.

AS FAR AS I'M AWARE, THERE IS NO OFFICIAL "US." YOU'RE NEVER AROUND!

THE GODS HAVE FORBIDDEN ME TO SPEND TIME WITH YOU, SINCE I DON'T HAVE A *HUMAN HOST.*

TONIGHT, I BREAK THE RULES TO DISCUSS *SHADOW MAGIC.* YOU AND CARTER ARE RIGHT TO SEEK APOPHIS'S SHADOW.

WE GODS HIDE OUR SHADOWS BECAUSE THEY CAN BE USED TO DESTROY US.

BUT THE SAME MAGIC THAT CAN BE USED TO DESTROY OUR SOULS CAN ALSO BE USED TO *REBOOT* THEM.

I KNOW BES'S SACRIFICE HAS WEIGHED ON YOU. SHADOW MAGIC COULD *REVIVE* HIM.

The souls of the dead started stretching, caught by a huge gust of wind.

UH-OH. TIME'S UP. HE'S COME FOR ME.

MY GREAT-GRANDFATHER, *SHU.*

WHOOSH

Shu was one of those ridiculous godly names I'd heard before.

AH. THE GOD OF FLIP-FLOPS. NO, WAIT. LEAKY BALLOONS. NO--

AIR! GOD OF THE AIR!

FRATERNIZING WITH A MORTAL GIRL? THIS IS THE *FINAL INSULT*, BOY!

I remembered the story of Nut and Geb, the sky and earth. Ra had commanded Nut's father, Shu, to keep the two lovers apart so they would never have children who might someday usurp Ra's throne.

That strategy hadn't worked, but apparently Shu was still trying.

I DON'T REMEMBER YOU WEARING A PILOT'S OUTFIT.

I'D PREFER TO BE *INVISIBLE*, THANK YOU VERY MUCH. BUT YOU MORTALS HAVE POLLUTED THE AIR SO BADLY, IT'S GETTING HARDER AND HARDER.

HAVEN'T YOU PEOPLE HEARD OF SPARE-THE-AIR DAYS? CARPOOLING? HYBRID ENGINES? AND DON'T GET ME STARTED ON *COWS*!

DID YOU KNOW THAT EVERY COW BELCHES AND FARTS OVER A HUNDRED GALLONS OF METHANE A DAY?

THERE ARE ONE AND A HALF BILLION COWS IN THE WORLD. DO YOU HAVE ANY IDEA WHAT THAT DOES TO MY RESPIRATORY SYSTEM?

PUFF PUFF

Shu's wind had blown the dance hall gazebo down. Hopefully none of the mortals had seen anything.

A golden light caught my attention.

EH?

A horde of ghosts, a blustery wind god, and now a portal!

SO MUCH FOR BEING *NORMAL* FOR A NIGHT.

On the other side, I could make out faint images of a subterranean city.

The First Nome.

Portals don't just appear randomly. Whoever had summoned it really must have wanted to talk to me.

I THINK THIS ONE'S FOR ME.

SADIE, I'M GOING TO STRANGLE YOU.

?

YOU HEARD ABOUT *DALLAS.* I'M SORRY--

Zia Rashid. Fire elementalist, and deputy to the Chief Lector.

EVERYONE HAS HEARD ABOUT DALLAS.

THE REBELS ARE ALREADY BLAMING YOU FOR THEIR DEATHS.

*The rebels. Last spring, the worst villains in the House of Life formed a **hit squad** to destroy Brooklyn House.*

*We **beat** them, but they swore to fight us another day.*

THEY'VE COME BACK EVEN STRONGER, TURNING OUR FRIENDS AGAINST US. DALLAS WAS ONE OF OUR LAST ALLIES.

FOLLOW ME THROUGH THE HALL OF AGES. THERE IS *MUCH* YOU NEED *TO SEE.*

The Hall of Ages.

Swirling curtains of multicolored light tell Egypt's history.

*The first section of light was gold--the **Age of the Gods.** Farther along, the **Old Kingdom** glowed silver, the **Middle Kingdom** was coppery brown, and so on.*

It's a looong hall.

At the end of the hall, the curtains of red light for the modern age changed to **dark purple**: the recent past.

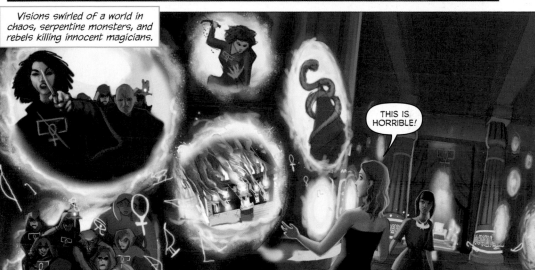

Visions swirled of a world in chaos, serpentine monsters, and rebels killing innocent magicians.

THIS IS HORRIBLE!

THEY DO NOT RECOGNIZE AMOS KANE AS CHIEF LECTOR. THEY DISTRUST THE KANES FOR USING THE POWER OF THE GODS. NOW THEY'RE SYSTEMATICALLY KILLING ANYONE WHO ALLIES WITH THE CHIEF LECTOR.

DID THEY... DID THE REBELS HAVE SOMETHING TO DO WITH DALLAS?

POSSIBLY.

LET'S NOT LINGER. YOUR UNCLE AMOS AWAITS US.

TRADITIONALLY, THE CHIEF LECTOR'S PLACE IS BESIDE THE PHARAOH'S THRONE.

BUT IN LIGHT OF RECENT EVENTS, HE'S SPENDING HIS TIME IN THE **WAR ROOM.**

THE MAP SHOWS US MOST OF OUR ENEMY'S MOVEMENTS ACROSS THE WORLD, AND ALLOWS US TO SEND OUR FORCES BY MAGIC TO WHERE THEY ARE NEEDED.

THE TOKENS STAND FOR ACTUAL FORCES.

A figurine burned at the sword of another.

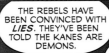

-≻SIGH≺- MORE LOSSES.

THE REBELS STRIKE WHEREVER WE ARE WEAKEST.

APOPHIS SENDS HIS DEMONS TO TERRORIZE OUR ALLIES. THE ATTACKS ARE **COORDINATED**.

THE FEAR GENERATED BY EACH ACT OF TERROR TURNS MORE AGAINST US.

THE REBELS HAVE BEEN CONVINCED WITH *LIES*. THEY'VE BEEN TOLD THE KANES ARE DEMONS.

HOW COULD THEY BE SO STUPID!

CHAOS IS *SEDUCTIVE*. THEY BELIEVE THEY CAN MAKE A NEW WORLD BETTER THAN THE OLD, AND THE CHANGE IS WORTH ANY PRICE--EVEN MASS ANNIHILATION.

APOPHIS HAS MADE PROMISES OF POWER, OR HE IS SIMPLY CONTROLLING THEIR MINDS.

Amos had been possessed by Chaos before, by the Chaos god Set.

Compared to Apophis, Set was a minor nuisance. Considering what Apophis could make a person do made me shudder.

YOU GAVE THEM AMNESTY WHEN THEY ATTACKED BROOKLYN HOUSE.

WE SHOULD'VE KILLED THE REBELS WHEN WE HAD THE CHANCE.

WE ARE SERVANTS OF *MA'AT*--ORDER AND JUSTICE. WE DON'T KILL OUR ENEMIES FOR THINGS THEY MIGHT DO IN THE FUTURE.

SOME MAY STILL BE TURNED BACK TO OUR SIDE.

A YOUNG DEFECTOR FROM RUSSIA HAS SUPPLIED US WITH INTELLIGENCE ON THE REBELS' MOVEMENTS.

THEY ARE RIGHT UNDER OUR NOSES, IN *ASWAN*.

FROM *ASWAN*, THEY WILL MARCH NORTH TO ATTACK US HERE IN THE FIRST NOME.

ATTACK THE FIRST NOME? HERE? THAT'D BE *SUICIDE*.

IT'S SURVIVED FOR FIVE THOUSAND YEARS!

SADIE, WE'RE *WEAKER* THAN YOU REALIZE.

WE DON'T HAVE THE NUMBERS TO HOLD OFF AGAINST OUR ENEMIES.

MANY OF OUR BEST MAGICIANS HAVE DISAPPEARED, POSSIBLY TO THE OTHER SIDE. WE'VE GOT SOME OLD MEN AND A FEW SCARED CHILDREN LEFT, PLUS ZIA AND ME.

WE WILL HAVE TO FIND STRENGTH THROUGH *OTHER MEANS*.

SET. I WILL FOLLOW THE PATH OF THE GODS.

MEMPHIS, TN.
PYRAMID SPORTS ARENA.
THOTH'S HOME BASE.

Freak brought us to a glassy black
pyramid along the Mississippi River.
It was the abandoned sports arena that
Thoth had appropriated for his home.

HMM.
MAYBE WE
SHOULD HAVE
GONE TO SADIE'S
DANCE AFTER
ALL.

MEMPHIS

CHAPTER 3

It was going great, until...

CARTER KANE, YOU ARE STUPIDLY PERSISTENT.

EH?

WHAM

AAIEE!

I recognized that voice.

HIDING BEHIND THE GODS WILL NOT SAVE YOU FROM WHAT MY MASTER BRINGS. APOPHIS WILL RISE!

Face of Horror—a demon from the Red Pyramid, and the secret mouthpiece of Apophis. We'd killed him in the shadow of the Washington Monument, but now he was back.

FACE OF HORROR? I KILLED YOU!

I GOT BETTER. MY MASTER HEALS ALL WOUNDS.

SURRENDER RA TO ME. I WILL SPARE YOU. YOU WILL RIDE THE SEA OF CHAOS. YOU WILL BE MASTER OF YOUR OWN DESTINY.

HAVE THE GODS PROMISED YOU ANYTHING AS FAIR?

CARTER KANE. YOU SHOULDN'T HAVE COME.

YOU'RE WELCOME. IT LOOKED LIKE YOU NEEDED HELP.

TO FIGHT THE DEMONS? THEY'LL BE BACK AT SUNRISE.

THEY'VE BEEN ATTACKING AT DUSK AND DAWN FOR THE PAST TWO WEEKS.

I IMAGINE THE OTHER GODS HAVEN'T COME TO MY RESCUE BECAUSE THEY'RE HAVING SIMILAR PROBLEMS. *RA WAS RECENTLY BROUGHT BACK*, AS YOU MAY RECALL.

THE SUN GOD MUST BE GUARDED ON HIS NIGHTLY JOURNEY. THAT TAKES A LOT OF *GODPOWER*.

SORRY, MY BAD. WELL, PARTLY. SADIE HELPED.

NOW THAT YOU'RE HERE, YOU MAY AS WELL COME INSIDE.

I THINK YOU'LL FIND MY HEADQUARTERS MUCH IMPROVED SINCE YOUR LAST VISIT.

THERE'S MUCH TO DISCUSS. AND YOU HAVE TO TRY MY BARBECUE!

I'll say this for Thoth. He knew how to decorate a pyramid.

INSTANT REPLAY
THOTH'S GOT WIIINGS

28-0

I KNEW SOONER OR LATER YOU'D COME TO THE CONCLUSION THAT YOUR ONLY HOPE OF VICTORY WAS A *SHADOW EXECRATION*.

YOU MEAN IT'S A REAL THING? WHAT IS IT, AND HOW DO WE PERFORM IT?

KNOWLEDGE OF ANY VALUE CAN'T BE GIVEN. IT MUST BE *SOUGHT* AND *EARNED*.

YOU'RE A TEACHER NOW, CARTER. YOU SHOULD KNOW THIS.

I CAN GUIDE YOU A LITTLE.

BUT YOU'LL HAVE TO CONNECT THE FRECKLES, AS THEY SAY.

DOTS.

RIGHT. THE OTHER GODS THINK I'M A SELLOUT. OVER THE CENTURIES, I'VE DIVULGED TOO MANY SECRETS TO MANKIND. I TAUGHT YOU THE ART OF WRITING, OF MAGIC. I FOUNDED THE HOUSE OF LIFE.

THAT'S WHY MAGICIANS STILL HONOR YOU. HELP US ONE MORE TIME.

YOUR OTHER OPTION IS NOT TO HELP US AND LET APOPHIS DESTROY THE WORLD.

POINT TAKEN. THERE IS A WAY YOU COULD FIND THE SHADOW'S LOCATION.

"LONG AGO, WHEN I WAS YOUNG AND NAIVE, I WROTE A FIELD STUDY CALLED *THE BOOK OF THOTH*.

"IT DESCRIBED EVERY FORM EACH GOD CAN TAKE, THEIR MOST SECRET HIDING PLACES--ALL SORTS OF EMBARRASSING DETAILS.

"I NEVER MEANT FOR HUMANS TO READ THE BOOK, BUT IT WAS *STOLEN* IN ANCIENT TIMES BY A CRAFTY AND MURDEROUS MAGICIAN.

"DOES THE NAME *SETNE* RING A BELL? IT SHOULD!

"SETNE WAS QUITE THE EVIL GENIUS. THE MOST DUPLICITOUS, CRAFTY, AND BRILLIANT MAGICIAN TO HAVE LIVED.

"BORN AS PRINCE KHAEMWASET, HEIR TO THE THRONE OF RAMSES, HE BATTLED MONSTERS, ADVENTURED IN THE DUAT, CONQUERED GODS, AND BROKE INTO SACRED TOMBS. HE CREATED CURSES THAT COULDN'T BE LIFTED AND UNEARTHED SECRETS THAT SHOULD HAVE STAYED BURIED.

"HE'D STOP AT NOTHING TO POSSESS THE SECRETS OF THE UNIVERSE. HE WANTED TO BE A GOD, YOU SEE-- NOT THE EYE OF A GOD, A FULL-FLEDGED IMMORTAL.

"SETNE USED MY BOOK TO FORMULATE A NUMBER OF SPELLS, INCLUDING THE *SHADOW EXECRATION*.

"FORTUNATELY HE DIED BEFORE HE COULD TAKE FULL ADVANTAGE OF IT."

SHLUK!

IF YOU NEED THE SPELL TO DEFEAT APOPHIS, YOU MIGHT BE ABLE TO CONVINCE SETNE TO TEACH YOU THE ENCHANTMENT AND LEAD YOU TO THE SHADOW OF APOPHIS.

BUT HOW? HE'S DEAD!

"DEATH WAS NOT THE END FOR SETNE. HE'S CONTINUED TO CAUSE TROUBLE FOR THOUSANDS OF YEARS IN THE UNDERWORLD, AS A *SPIRIT!*"

OSIRIS SENTENCED HIM TO OBLIVION MANY TIMES, BUT SETNE ALWAYS MANAGED TO EVADE PUNISHMENT.

HE GOT A LIGHTER SENTENCE, WON APPEALS, MADE PLEA BARGAINS, OR HE SIMPLY ESCAPED.

RECENTLY, *YOUR FATHER* BECAME OSIRIS.

HE'S BEEN CRACKING DOWN ON REBELLIOUS GHOSTS, TRYING TO RESTORE *MA'AT* TO AN UNDERWORLD INCREASINGLY BENDING TO CHAOS.

NOW SETNE IS SCHEDULED FOR A *NEW TRIAL*. HE WILL COME BEFORE YOUR FATHER *TOMORROW* AND SETNE WILL NEED TO MAKE A DEAL TO SURVIVE.

GO TO THE HALL OF JUDGMENT. INTERVENE IN THE TRIAL. CONVINCE SETNE TO SHOW YOU WHERE HE HID MY BOOK OF THOTH, LEAD YOU TO APOPHIS'S SHADOW, AND TEACH YOU HOW TO DESTROY IT.

IF HE DOESN'T ESCAPE, KILL YOU, OR BETRAY YOU, HE MAY DECIDE TO HELP YOU. NOW--

--IT'S ALMOST DAWN. YOU TWO HAD BETTER LEAVE BEFORE THE DEMONS RETURN. GOOD LUCK.

AND BY ALL MEANS, GIVE SETNE MY REGARDS!

IF YOU LIVE LONG ENOUGH TO DO SO, OF COURSE.

Walt and I held on to the boat on our way back to Brooklyn.

Maybe it was lack of sleep after a night of fighting and conversation with Thoth, but Walt was not looking healthy.

IT'S *THE CURSE*. I'VE NOT GOT LONG TO LIVE.

UNTIL SUNSET TOMORROW, AT THE VERY LATEST.

I WON'T LET IT STOP ME FROM HELPING YOU BEAT APOPHIS.

ANUBIS THINKS THERE'S A WAY TO EXTEND MY LIFE.

IT'S NOT A CURE, AND THERE COULD BE SIDE EFFECTS. YOU MIGHT NOT LIKE IT; SADIE MIGHT NOT LIKE IT.

HE'S BEEN HELPING ME MAKE SENSE OF *MY POWERS*.

YOUR POWERS...ARE YOU TALKING ABOUT THAT DEATH TOUCH YOU USED ON THE CRIOSPHINX IN DALLAS?

-÷GASP!÷-

IT'S STILL EARLY MORNING. I DON'T SEE ANY INITIATES EATING BREAKFAST OR PREPARING FOR "MAGIC PROBLEM-SOLVING 101."

WHERE IS EVERYBODY?

A weird creature was waiting for us. It spoke with Sadie's voice:

WE'VE SHIPPED OFF TO EGYPT, JUST SOUTH OF CAIRO.

Sadie had the harebrained idea to create the **perfect shabti** to be her avatar and do all her chores, like a remote-controlled robot. Not being much of an artist, Sadie had fashioned a vaguely human figure out of flowerpots.

THERE'S AN EMERGENCY AT THE FIRST NOME. ZIA BROUGHT ME HERE AT AMOS'S CALL. THE HOUSE OF LIFE IS FACING A CIVIL WAR.

STOP SMILING! I CAN **SEE** YOU, CARTER. OH--AND, UH, HULLO, WALT.

SARAH JACOBI AND HER FORCES ARE MARCHING ON US, TIMING THEIR ATTACK TO APOPHIS'S RISE. I CALLED THE INITIATES HERE TO DEFEND THE HALL OF AGES.

WE'RE TRAINING! JOIN US HERE!

WISH WE COULD, SADIE.

WE CONSULTED WITH THOTH. ALL HIS SHADOW MAGIC RECIPES WERE STOLEN EONS AGO BY A ROGUE MAGICIAN NAMED SETNE. WE'RE GOING TO *SUMMON A BOAT* TO *THE UNDERWORLD* TO TALK SETNE'S GHOST INTO SHOWING US WHERE THEY'RE HIDDEN.

THE *LAND OF THE DEAD*, EH? MAYBE I SHOULD JOIN YOU THERE. I WANT TO VISIT BES.

DON'T FRET. I THINK IT WILL HELP US WITH OUR *SHADOW PROJECT*.

RIGHT, I'LL MEET YOU TWO AT THE HALL OF JUDGMENT BEFORE SUNSET TONIGHT. TA!

Opening a portal can be easy when you ask the right goddess. I sauntered over to a half-destroyed shrine to Isis.

YOO-HOO, ISIS? ANYONE HOME?

I ANSWER THE CALL.

IF IT ISN'T MY GOOD FRIEND WHO DECIDES WHOM I CAN AND CAN'T DATE.

ARE YOU SPEAKING OF ANUBIS? SADIE, THERE ARE *RULES*.

PROXIMITY TO THE GODS IS *DANGEROUS*. IT MUST BE REGULATED WITH UTMOST CARE. YOU KNOW THIS. YOUR UNCLE IS STILL TAINTED FROM HIS EXPERIENCE WITH SET.

EVEN *THAT ONE* STRUGGLES WITH IT.

Zia? She's never shown interest in the path of the gods. What was Isis talking about?

IF YOU JOIN WITH ME, YOU'LL *UNDERSTAND*.

IT'S TIME WE UNITE AGAIN AND COMBINE OUR STRENGTH.

SOON. FOR NOW I NEED TO BE SURE MY DECISIONS ARE MY OWN.

BEFORE THEN, I NEED HELP WITH A *PORTAL*.

I imagined wheelchairs, IV poles, and all the forgotten old gods of Egypt situated on a boiling *lake of fire*.

The House of Rest, retirement home to the gods.

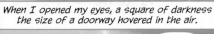

When I opened my eyes, a square of darkness the size of a doorway hovered in the air.

IT IS **DONE**.

GOOD LUCK. I WILL AWAIT YOUR CALL.

AMOS, I JUST SPOKE TO CARTER. I'VE SUMMONED A PORTAL TO MEET CARTER IN THE UNDERWORLD.

WHAT DO YOU THINK? ARE OUR INITIATES PREPARED TO FACE OFF AGAINST THE WORST HIT SQUAD THE HOUSE OF LIFE HAS TO OFFER?

OUR ADDED NUMBERS ARE ENCOURAGING. THANK YOU, SADIE.

I WISH YOU WOULD STAY HERE WITH US, BUT I KNOW HOW STUBBORN **KANES** CAN BE WHEN WE PUT OUR MINDS TO SOMETHING.

STILL, IT'S NOT SAFE TO TRAVEL ALONE, EVEN BY PORTAL.

ZIA!

YES, CHIEF LECTOR?

PLEASE ACCOMPANY MY NIECE TO THE UNDERWORLD.

Zia looked apprehensive.

CHEER UP, IT'LL BE A **LAUGH**. QUICK TRIP TO THE NETHERWORLD, FIERY LAKE OF DOOM. WHAT COULD GO WRONG?

SUNNY ACRES
RETIREMENT HOME
FOR THE GODS.

Carter and I had been to the retirement home
for senile gods before. It was a sorry sight.
The head nurse was *Tawaret*. All the residents
received her care, but the one who got the
most attention was dear old Bes.

ONE MORE
BITE, BES. YOU
CAN DO IT.

CHAPTER 4

EAT YOUR LUNCH.

FWOOSH!

HE WAS HERE. TRAPPED FOR EONS.

ZIA, HAVE YOU GONE MAD?!

THAT WAS A PERFECTLY INNOCENT WHEELCHAIR.

EH??

MISERABLE AND ALONE. FORCED TO ABDICATE HIS THRONE.

HE WAS TRAPPED HERE WITHOUT THE WILL TO LIVE.

The scarab amulet around her neck glowed with heat.

The amulet had been given to her by Ra after the battle of Brooklyn House six months ago.

SADIE!

I HAVEN'T SEEN YOU IN AGES! IS EVERYTHING OKAY?

NOT QUITE. THE APOCALYPSE IS COMING.

TAWARET, I'D LIKE YOU TO MEET MY FRIEND ZIA.

HELLO, MY DEAR. I'M TAWARET, HEAD CARETAKER HERE IN THE HOUSE OF REST.

WE'RE HERE TO SEE BES. IS HE...?

RIGHT THIS WAY. I WAS JUST FINISHING HIS AFTERNOON FEEDING.

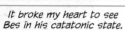
It broke my heart to see Bes in his catatonic state.

DEAR BES, WE'RE GOING TO **HELP** YOU.

SADIE THINKS WE CAN RESTORE BES'S SOUL WITH SHADOW MAGIC.

IF WE CAN RESTORE HIS SHEUT TO HIS BODY, HE COULD BE HIMSELF AGAIN! BUT WE NEED TO FIND IT FIRST.

YOU ARE THE PERSON WHO WAS CLOSEST TO HIM. I'M WONDERING IF HE EVER SHOWED YOU HIS **SHADOW**.

Tawaret blushed.

WHAT YOU ASK IS VERY INTIMATE.

I SAW HIS SHADOW ONCE, IN **SAIS**, A CITY ON THE NILE DELTA.

☆ SAÏS

"SAIS WAS THE HOME OF OUR FRIEND THE HUNTING GODDESS **NEITH**. SHE LIKED TO INVITE BES AND ME ON HER HUNTING EXCURSIONS. WE WOULD FLUSH PREY FOR HER TO CATCH.

"ONE NIGHT AFTER DINNER, BES AND I SAT ALONE ON THE WALLS OF NEITH'S TEMPLE, WATCHING THE MOON RISE OVER THE NILE.

"I FELT SO CLOSE TO HIM. JUST FOR A MOMENT, I LOOKED AT THE WALL NEXT TO US, AND I SAW BES'S SHADOW IN THE TORCHLIGHT.

"NORMALLY GODS GUARD THEIR SHADOWS CLOSELY. HE MUST'VE TRUSTED ME A GREAT DEAL TO REVEAL IT."

THIS IS A GOOD PLACE FOR ME TO LEAVE MY SHADOW.

THAT WAY IT CAN ALWAYS BE HAPPY. EVEN WHEN I'M NOT.

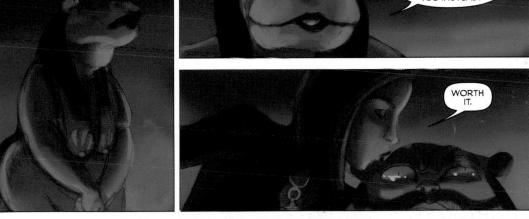

THAT NIGHT WAS A FEW THOUSAND YEARS AGO.

THE TEMPLE IS GONE. MOST OF THE LAND HAS REVERTED TO MARSHES.

HOWEVER-- YOU'RE BES'S FRIEND. IF YOU SEARCH THE AREA, HIS SHADOW MAY APPEAR TO YOU. AND IF *NEITH* IS STILL AROUND, SHE MIGHT BE ABLE TO HELP. THAT IS, IF SHE DOESN'T *HUNT* YOU INSTEAD.

WORTH IT.

I saw a boat crossing the lake of fire.

LOOKS LIKE OUR RIDE OUT OF HERE.

CARTER HAS A STEAMBOAT?

IT'S SOMETHING OF A FAMILY HEIRLOOM...

EGYPTIAN QUEEN

THE *EGYPTIAN QUEEN* BELONGED TO OUR PARENTS WHEN THEY WERE ALIVE. WE CAN SUMMON IT ONCE A YEAR!

EGYPTIAN QUEEN

The only drawback to the *Egyptian Queen* is its captain.

WELCOME ABOARD, LADY KANE.

I AM AT YOUR SERVICE.

Bloodstained Blade had followed our orders in the past, but that was little comfort. He'd **slit our throats** if he ever got the opportunity!

DINNER IS PREPARED.

LORDS *CARTER* AND *WALT* AWAIT YOU IN THE STATEROOM.

On the other hand, we needed to get to the Hall of Judgment.

I was hungry and thirsty, and I could endure a twenty-minute voyage if it meant enjoying a chilled Ribena and a plate of tandoori chicken with naan.

EGYPTIAN QUEEN

WALT, YOUR CURSE!

He was getting weaker.

UH, HI, ZIA.

CARTER. HOW...ARE THINGS?

Other kids checked their cell phones, but for the last six months I'd been obsessed with a birdbath. Zia and I liked to **scry**-- a magical way to get face time with each other.

This was the first time they'd been together **in person** in six months. Awkward!

PAT PAT

We didn't get far into dinner before a loudspeaker crackled with Bloodstained Blade's voice:

MY LORDS AND LADIES, WE HAVE REACHED THE HALL OF JUDGMENT.

SETNE, ALSO KNOWN AS PRINCE KHAEMWASET--

--YOU STAND ACCUSED OF HEINOUS CRIMES! YOU HAVE BLASPHEMED AGAINST THE GODS FOUR THOUSAND AND NINETY-TWO TIMES.

YOU HAVE USED MAGIC FOR EVIL PURPOSES, INCLUDING TWENTY-THREE MURDERS...

...AND ONE INCIDENT WHERE YOU WERE PAID TO KILL WITH MAGIC.

YOU PLOTTED AGAINST THREE SEPARATE PHARAOHS AND YOU TRIED TO OVERTHROW THE HOUSE OF LIFE ON SIX OCCASIONS.

MOST GRIEVOUS OF ALL, YOU ROBBED THE TOMBS OF THE DEAD TO STEAL BOOKS OF MAGIC.

HOW DO YOU PLEAD?

NOT GUILTY!

THE MURDERS WERE IN SELF-DEFENSE!

THE MURDERS FOR HIRE-- SELF-DEFENSE FOR MY *EMPLOYER*.

LOOK, OSIRIS, A HANDSOME, INTELLIGENT JUDGMENT GOD LIKE YOU HAS TO FEEL OVERWORKED AND UNDERAPPRECIATED. I FEEL FOR YOU, I REALLY DO.

YOU'VE GOT BETTER THINGS TO DO THAN DIG UP MY OLD HISTORY. BESIDES, ALL THESE CHARGES-- I ANSWERED TO THEM ALREADY IN MY PREVIOUS TRIALS.

SILENCE! YOU USE *DIVINE WORDS* AND ATTEMPT TO INFLUENCE MY MIND, WARPING THE MOST SACRED MAGIC OF *MA'AT*.

EVEN IN YOUR BINDINGS YOU ARE DANGEROUS.

YOU HAVE BEEN SENTENCED TO OBLIVION MORE THAN ONCE. THE FIRST TIME YOU MANAGED TO PLEAD FOR A REDUCED SENTENCE, VOLUNTEERING TO SERVE THE PHARAOH WITH YOUR MAGIC--

--YET YOU ESCAPED EN ROUTE. YOU KILLED YOUR GUARDS AND SPENT THE NEXT THREE HUNDRED YEARS SOWING CHAOS ACROSS EGYPT.

AS HOST OF OSIRIS, I WILL NOT TOLERATE THE EXISTENCE OF A VILLAIN LIKE YOU, EVEN AS A SPIRIT.

SERVANTS OF OSIRIS'S COURT-- READY HIS HEART!

WE WILL WEIGH IT AGAINST THE *FEATHER OF TRUTH*.

IF HIS HEART IS SHOWN TO BE WICKED, WE WILL FEED IT TO THE *DEVOURER OF SOULS*.

GRRR...

DAD! PLEASE, DON'T!

HEY, POOCHIEKINS!

PLEASE DO NOT CALL THE DEVOURER OF SOULS "POOCHIEKINS"! SADIE AND CARTER, I'M *WORKING*. WHAT ARE YOU DOING HERE, MY CHILDREN?

DAD, PLEASE, WE NEED CUSTODY OF SETNE.

WE'VE FIGURED OUT A WAY TO DEFEAT APOPHIS USING A SHADOW EXECRATION. BUT ONLY SETNE KNOWS WHERE THE SPELL CAN BE ACCESSED.

YOU WANT ANSWERS FROM THIS WRETCH? GUARDS, LET HIM HOLD THE FEATHER OF TRUTH WHILE HE EXPLAINS HIMSELF.

SPEAK TRUTHFULLY, GHOST, OR THE FEATHER WILL INCINERATE YOU.

IT'S TRUE. I STOLE THE *BOOK OF THOTH* IN MY MORTAL LIFE. THE BOOK EXPLAINS HOW TO FIND THE SHADOW OF APOPHIS, HOW TO CAPTURE IT, AND HOW TO CAST THE EXECRATION.

TELL MY CHILDREN WHERE IT'S HIDDEN.

NOT THAT EASY. WHILE I WAS ALIVE I HID THE *BOOK OF THOTH* AND GUARDED IT WITH CURSES THAT ONLY *I* CAN UNDO.

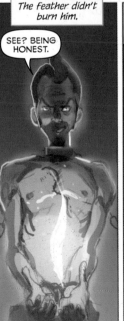

The feather didn't burn him.

SEE? BEING HONEST.

I'M THE ONLY ONE WHO CAN RETRIEVE IT. THERE ARE TRAPS, CURSES...AND YOU'LL NEED MY HELP DECIPHERING THE NOTES. THE SPELL IS COMPLICATED!

NO, ABSOLUTELY NOT. I WOULD NEVER RELEASE YOU, ESPECIALLY NOT TO MY CHILDREN. YOU ARE A SERVANT OF CHAOS.

I'M A LOT OF THINGS, BUT A SERVANT OF THE SNAKE? NO. I DON'T WANT THE WORLD DESTROYED. THERE'S NOTHING IN THAT FOR ME.

IF I CAUSE YOU ANY TROUBLE, YOU CAN TIE ME UP LIKE A CAMEL AT MARKET.

I WON'T TRY TO ESCAPE-- AT LEAST NOT UNTIL I LEAD YOU TO THE BOOK OF THOTH AND THEN GET YOU SAFELY TO THE SHADOW OF APOPHIS.

FOUR OF US, ONE OF HIM.

HE'S KILLED HIS GUARDS BEFORE....

SO WE'LL BE MORE CAREFUL. TOGETHER, ALL OF US SHOULD BE ABLE TO KEEP HIM UNDER CONTROL.

OH, EXCEPT... SEE, SADIE'S GOT HER LITTLE *SIDE TASK*, DOESN'T SHE?

SADIE'S GOTTA FIND THE SHADOW OF BES. AND ACTUALLY, IT'S A GOOD IDEA.

HOW DID YOU...?

DON'T BE SURPRISED, PRINCESS. YOU SERIOUSLY NEED TO WORK ON YOUR MENTAL DEFENSES. READING YOUR MIND IS WAY TOO EASY.

PERFORMING A SHADOW EXECRATION IN REVERSE COULD RESTORE BES AND BE A GOOD TEST OF THE MAGIC BEFORE IT'S TIME TO FACE APOPHIS!

SADIE, HE'S TRYING TO DIVIDE US.

YOU CAN SAVE BES AFTERWARD.

...

Hapi is the god of the Nile, provider of bountiful harvests and protector of the Nile.

WHY, YES, I AM HAPPY! I'M ALWAYS HAPPY, BECAUSE I'M HAPI! ARE YOU HAPPY?

UHH...YES! WE'RE HAVING A VERY HAPPY DAY.

BUT WHAT'S GOING TO MAKE US EVEN HAPPIER IS A TRIP TO THE SERAPEUM OF APIS.

THE SERAPEUM?

THAT'S PRETTY FAR INLAND. IF YOU ARE PLANNING TO GET THERE BY BOAT, IT'S GOING TO BE A CHALLENGE.

APOPHIS'S MINIONS ARE EVEN *LARGER* AS YOU GET CLOSER TO GIZA! IT'S BEEN QUITE A WEEK CLEARING THEM OUT.

AND IF YOU'RE RELYING ON A DEMON TO CAPTAIN YOUR SHIP, YOU'RE ALREADY OFF TO A ROUGH START.

MAY I SUGGEST AN ALTERNATE FORM OF TRAVEL?

Hapi pulled two weird seeds off his head that looked like fish eggs.

THEY'RE *HAPI PILLS.* SWALLOW ONE EACH AND I GUARANTEE YOU'LL HAVE A TRIP! WHEREVER YOU IMAGINE.

I know I'm going to sound like a public service announcement here, but for all you kids at home: if somebody offers you Hapi pills, just say "No!"

They tasted even worse than they looked.

Within a minute I began to feel queasy. And then...

CARTER, YOU'RE MELTING!

Y-Y-YOU TOO...

Being *liquidated* is not fun.

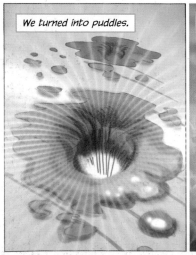

We turned into puddles.

I felt myself evaporating and moving inland at incredible speed.

I couldn't exactly see, but I could feel the movement and the heat of the desert as we were pushed west.

I focused my molecules on one mantra: Serapeum of Apis, Serapeum of Apis.

I materialized somewhere else, gasping for air.

HEY, WATCH THE SHOES, KID!

HUK...

BARF!

NEVER... AGAIN.

AW, C'MON! THAT WAS A SMOOTH TRIP! LOOK, EVEN YOUR SHIP MADE IT.

For some reason, a huge slimy tarp of fish scales was hanging off the pilot's house like a snagged parachute.

OH, GODS OF EGYPT--

PLEASE DON'T LET THAT BE HAPI'S LOINCLOTH.

SERAPEUM

THE BOOK OF THOTH'S UNDERGROUND. FOLLOW ME!

YOU'RE GOING TO LOVE THIS PLACE!

I did not love this place.

The hall was musty, dark, and lined with sarcophagi much too large for humans.

I BUILT ALL THIS, IN MY MORTAL LIFE AS *PRINCE KHAEMWASET.*

THESE ARE THE BURIAL CHAMBERS FOR THE SACRED *APIS BULL.*

HE HAD THE *PERFECT LIFE.* ALL THE FOOD HE COULD EAT, A HAREM OF COWS--EVERY PERK. ONLY HAD TO SHOW HIMSELF IN PUBLIC A FEW TIMES A YEAR FOR BIG FESTIVALS.

WHEN HE TURNED TWENTY-FIVE, HE GOT SLAUGHTERED IN A BIG CEREMONY, MUMMIFIED LIKE A KING, AND PUT DOWN HERE. THEN A NEW BULL TOOK HIS PLACE. A GREAT GIG!

KILLED AT TWENTY-FIVE. SOUNDS AWESOME.

NOT IMPRESSED? WAIT UNTIL YOU SEE THE SHRINE OF APIS.

Setne led us to a dead end and spoke a spell.

TIME FOR THE BEHIND-THE-SCENES TOUR.

The dead end disappeared, revealing a hidden room.

SHOWTIME, KIDS.

Three tons of laser-blasting bovine craziness versus a raging hawk god. Who do you think would win?

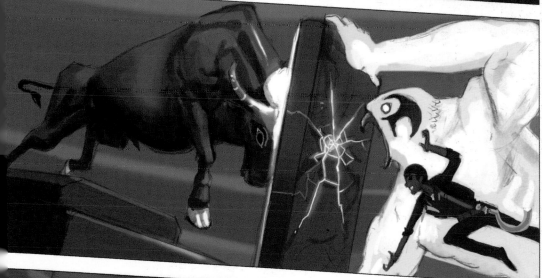

CARTER!

So much for the avatar.

ZIA, SAVE YOURSELF! *RUN!*

NOT ZIA.

I AM KHEPRI, THE RISING SUN.

I WILL NOT BE DENIED.

There was no question Zia had used the *path of the gods.*

TOO HOT TO HANDLE, EH? MOST WHO CALL ON THE POWER OF RA SPONTANEOUSLY COMBUST!

AT LEAST YOU'VE GOT THE BOOK OF THOTH! IF SHE DIES, IT WASN'T FOR NOTHING....

IF SHE DIES, I WILL--

YOU'LL WHAT? EXECRATE ME?

YOU STILL NEED ME AROUND, PAL. WHO ELSE WILL GET YOU THROUGH THE LAND OF THE DEMONS IN ONE PIECE?

WHICH REMINDS ME, WE NEED TO GET BACK TO THE RIVER OF NIGHT, ASAP!

HOW ABOUT I GO TELL YOUR CAPTAIN WHERE WE'RE HEADING. DO I HAVE YOUR PERMISSION TO GIVE HIM ORDERS?

WITH PLEASURE!

Zia's fever subsided.

I kissed her forehead and I stayed by her side, holding her hand.

I was distraught. He didn't even have to use divine words.

FINE, JUST GET OUT OF MY SIGHT.

I felt a lurch as the boat entered the *Duat*.

CREEAK...

LORD KANE, IT'S TIME TO DIE.

BLOODSTAINED BLADE?! BACK DOWN, THAT'S AN ORDER.

NEW ORDERS: *KILL CARTER KANE*. TAKE HIM TO THE LAND OF DEMONS.

MAKE SURE IT'S A *ONE-WAY TRIP*.

Walt and I made our way upriver on the back of **Philip of Macedonia.**
In the distance, I saw a clearing with a few clumps of mud brick sticking above the grass like rotten teeth.
WE'RE HERE. THE ***RUINS OF SAIS***. SOMEWHERE NEARBY, IS BES'S SHADOW.

CHAPTER 6

On the shore, a symbol had been scratched into the dirt.

TWO ARROWS AND A SHIELD.

THIS IS NEITH'S SYMBOL.

SHE RULED SAIS IN ANCIENT TIMES. MAYBE SHE CAN HELP US NOW.

MY CURSE... DON'T HAVE MUCH TIME.

I...CAN MANAGE IT. SADIE, IF I DIE FOR SOMETHING I BELIEVE IN, THAT'S OKAY WITH ME.

BUT DEATH DOESN'T HAVE TO BE THE END. I'VE BEEN TALKING WITH *ANUBIS*, AND--

GODS OF EGYPT, NOT THAT AGAIN!

PLEASE DON'T TALK ABOUT HIM.

I KNOW EXACTLY WHAT HE'S BEEN TELLING YOU.

YOU... DO?

HE'S BEEN PREPARING YOU FOR THE AFTERLIFE. YOU'LL DIE A NOBLE DEATH, GET A SPEEDY TRIAL, AND GO STRAIGHT INTO ANCIENT EGYPTIAN PARADISE.

NO, IT'S JUST-- YOU DON'T UNDERSTAND. IT'S NOT LIKE THAT.

WELL, THEN WHAT IS IT LIKE? I DON'T NEED ANOTHER PERSON I CAN'T BE WITH.

SHRINK PHILIP BACK TO SHABTI SIZE AND LET'S GO, EH?

We came upon a clear path of mud-brick ruins.

YOU MUST BE *NEITH*. I UNDERSTAND YOU'RE A FRIEND OF BES AND TAWARET'S.

SADIE KANE. *THE OTHERS* TOLD ME YOU WOULD COME.

RUSSIAN MAGICIANS. AFTER THAT, A FEW DEMONS CAME BY. THEY ALL WANTED TO KILL YOU.

I DESTROYED THEM.

MORTALS, MAGICIANS, DEMONS, THE TAX COLLECTORS... ANYONE WHO INVADES MY TERRITORY PAYS. I TAKE TROPHIES.

Neith dug out a necklace strung with ragged squares of cloth-- denim, linen, silk.

DO YOU THINK ME *CRUEL*? OH, YES, I COLLECT THE *POCKETS* OF MY ENEMIES.

The goddess was a nutter. Unfortunately, we needed her help.

I KNOW WHAT YOU'RE LOOKING FOR.

BES'S *SHEUT* DWELLS IN MY REALM-- IN THE *SHADOWS OF ANCIENT TIMES*.

IN THE WHAT NOW?

Neith shot a glowing arrow into the sky.

As Neith's arrow sailed upward, the air rippled.

A shock wave spread across the landscape.

Where the mud-brick ruins had been, a proud temple now stood.

WE'RE IN THE PAST?

A **SHADOW** OF IT.

A MEMORY.

IT MAY BE YOUR BURIAL GROUND, UNLESS YOU SURVIVE **THE HUNT**.

YOU MEAN-- **YOU** HUNT **US**? BES IS YOUR FRIEND. YOU SHOULD BE HELPING US!

WE'RE NOT YOUR ENEMY! APOPHIS MEANS TO DESTROY THE WORLD TOMORROW MORNING.

I'VE SEEN THE END COMING FOR EONS.

YOU SOFT MORTALS HAVE IGNORED THE WARNING SIGNS, WHILE I'VE PREPARED AN UNDERGROUND BUNKER STOCKPILED WITH FOOD, CLEAN WATER, AND ENOUGH AMMUNITION TO HOLD OFF ANY **ARMY**!

EVADE ME UNTIL SUNSET, AND I'LL FIGHT WITH YOU AGAINST THE SERPENT. YOU CAN EVEN LIVE IN MY BUNKER IF YOU CHOOSE.

I'LL EVEN GIVE YOU A FIVE-MINUTE HEAD START.

BUT I SHOULD WARN YOU: I NEVER LOSE. WHEN I KILL YOU, I'LL TAKE YOUR POCKETS!

YOU DRIVE A HARD BARGAIN, BUT FINE.

COME ON, WALT!!

WE SPLIT UP AND BUY TIME. WE CAN SHARE THOUGHTS THROUGH THE AMULETS, YES?

AND THEY CAN TELEPORT US TO EACH OTHER'S SIDE, RIGHT?

I DESIGNED THEM FOR THAT, BUT--

TWO TARGETS ARE HARDER TO CATCH THAN ONE.

IF WE GET IN TROUBLE, ONE OF US CAN WILL THE OTHER ONE OUT OF DANGER.

I was almost to Neith's temple when I heard Walt's voice in my mind:

SADIE, HELP!

I pictured Walt standing next to me, preferably without an arrow in him.

THANKS!

I SEE IT! BES'S SHADOW!

WALT, HOW DO WE CAPTURE IT?

YOU DON'T.

The air rippled as the magic shock wave contracted, transforming the landscape back to present-day Egypt.

The last walls of the temple were reduced to a pile of worn mud bricks, but the shadow of Bes was still visible against them, slowly fading as the sun went down.

Walt readied his magic wand, much to my dismay.

WE NEED TO CAPTURE BES'S SPIRIT BEFORE NIGHTFALL....

PUT AWAY YOUR WAND, WALT! USING MAGIC WILL KILL YOU!

AHEM.

ANUBIS?

I'M SORRY TO INTRUDE. BUT WALT--IT'S *TIME*. HAVE YOU MADE *YOUR DECISION*?

DIDN'T THE GODS PUT A RESTRAINING ORDER ON YOU?

STAY AWAY FROM WALT, *DEATH BOY!*

WALT WAS BORN UNDER THE SHADOW OF DEATH. THAT'S WHY WE UNDERSTAND EACH OTHER.

I'VE MADE... MY DECISION.... I CAN'T LEAVE HER.

NEITHER CAN I. BUT THE SHADOW, FIRST?

Walt pulled a handmade shabti of Bes out of his bag.

YES. BEFORE IT'S TOO LATE.

SADIE, WATCH WALT NOW.

YOU'LL NEED THE SAME ENCHANTMENT TO CAPTURE THE SERPENT'S SHADOW.

Walt chanted, and the shabti absorbed the shadow of Bes like a sponge soaking up liquid. The wax turned as black as *kohl*.

Walt spoke the last word of the spell:

HI-NEHM.*

*"Join together."

The hieroglyph for "join together" blazed silver against the dark wax.

With horrible certainty, I knew it would be the last spell Walt ever cast.

SHABTI AND SHADOW... BONDED...

SEND THE SHADOW BACK TO BES....

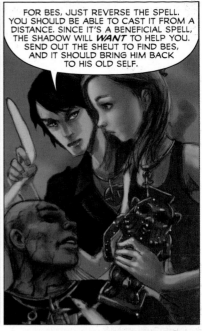

FOR BES, JUST REVERSE THE SPELL. YOU SHOULD BE ABLE TO CAST IT FROM A DISTANCE. SINCE IT'S A BENEFICIAL SPELL, THE SHADOW WILL *WANT* TO HELP YOU. SEND OUT THE SHEUT TO FIND BES, AND IT SHOULD BRING HIM BACK TO HIS OLD SELF.

I reversed the wording of an execration spell. Instead of erasing Bes from the world, I tried to draw him back into the picture, this time with permanent ink.

I imagined Bes as I had known him.

Chauffeur... savior... friend.

The wax statue disappeared.

WALT, DID IT WORK?

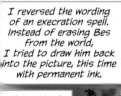

No answer.

Walt's eyes were closed. His forehead was rapidly cooling.

OH, PLEASE-- NO.

ANUBIS, DO SOMETHING!

ANUBIS?

ANUBIS!

THAT'S IT? YOU TAKE HIS SOUL AND LEAVE? I *HATE* YOU!

Suddenly, Walt opened his eyes.

-:GASP!:-

GO THROUGH THE GATE. IT WILL TAKE YOU TO CARTER. HE NEEDS YOUR HELP.

SADIE, HURRY. *YOU KNOW THE SPELL NOW.* IT WILL WORK ON THE SERPENT'S SHADOW.

His voice sounded clearer, free of pain-- but still weak.

I'LL MEET YOU AT THE FIRST NOME AT SUNRISE, IF YOU'RE SURE YOU DON'T HATE ME.

HATE YOU? WHY ON EARTH WOULD I HATE YOU?

LOOK.

I lowered my vision into the Duat.

OH NO, NO--

WHAT HAVE YOU DONE?

SADIE, IT'S ME--

--STILL ME--

--STILL ME. PLEASE, SADIE.

Too many puzzle pieces fell together at once. Walt was following the *path of Anubis.*

I'm not proud of how I acted, but I turned and fled, leaping straight through the doorway of darkness.

At the moment I didn't even care where it led, as long as it was away from that deathless creature I had thought I loved.

While Sadie was having her supernatural guy drama, I faced off against an ax-murdering riverboat captain dead set on changing his name to *Even-More-Bloodstained Blade*.

The *Egyptian Queen* weaved drunkenly in the current of the River of Night. I had to get control of the boat before we crashed!

CHAPTER 7

I ran for the wheelhouse.

No one was steering. I saw a dark strip up ahead--land. We were headed straight toward it.

RRRR!

ENOUGH!

I HAVE SERVED THE KANES TOO LONG!

WE ARE DONE!

YES, WE'RE DONE.

THANKS, ZIA.

THUNK!

NOW, WHERE'D THAT BACKSTABBING GHOST GO OFF TO?

The gangplank was lowering.

Setne strolled to the edge of the plank, waiting as the boat raced toward the black-sand beach.

IT'LL BE FINE, CARTER! I'LL BE RIGHT BACK!

EGYPTIAN QUEEN

TAS!*

AGH!

*"Bind!"

EGYPTIAN QUEEN

SPLOOSH!

Zia rubbed blue paste on the cuts, burns, and bruises that covered my upper body.

The gash mended. The wounds disappeared.

Inside my chest, I swear I could feel my ribs mending. I took a deep breath and was relieved to find it didn't hurt.

I CAN'T BELIEVE YOU GRANTED SETNE PERMISSION TO GIVE BLOODSTAINED BLADE ORDERS!

AND NOW WE'RE STRANDED IN THE LAND OF DEMONS, THE MOST DANGEROUS PART OF THE DUAT.

YEAH. MAYBE NOT MY BEST IDEA.

BONK

Our gift-wrapped ghost was trying to crawl away.

WE COULD LEAVE HIM LIKE THAT, BUT HE'S GOT THE BOOK OF THOTH.

NO HURRY. HE WON'T GET FAR. HOW ABOUT A PICNIC?

I LIKE THE WAY YOU THINK.

CARTER, ABOUT THE SERAPEUM AND MY CHANNELING OF RA'S POWER.

I WANTED TO TELL YOU, BUT I DIDN'T UNDERSTAND WHAT WAS HAPPENING TO ME. I WAS FRIGHTENED.

I WAS THE EYE OF HORUS. I UNDERSTAND.

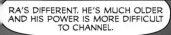

RA'S DIFFERENT. HE'S MUCH OLDER AND HIS POWER IS MORE DIFFICULT TO CHANNEL.

WHEN I TAP INTO RA'S POWER, I SENSE PANIC. HE FEELS IMPRISONED, HELPLESS.

REACHING OUT TO HIM IS LIKE TRYING TO SAVE SOMEBODY WHO'S DROWNING. THEY GRAB ON TO YOU AND TAKE YOU DOWN WITH THEM.

HIS POWER TRIES TO ESCAPE THROUGH ME AND I CAN BARELY CONTROL IT. EVERY TIME I BLACK OUT, IT GETS WORSE. RA WANTS ME TO BE HIS HOST. I FEAR I'M TOO WEAK TO CONTROL HIS POWER.

IN THE CATACOMBS WITH THE APIS BULL, I MIGHT'VE KILLED YOU.

BUT YOU DIDN'T. YOU SAVED MY LIFE! IF I'VE LEARNED ANYTHING WORKING WITH HORUS, IT'S ABOUT STRIKING A BALANCE.

YOU'RE THE KEY TO BRINGING HIM BACK!

SOMETIMES YOU HAVE TO FOLLOW YOUR HEART.

I'd never pictured my first date being on a bone-littered riverbank in the Land of Demons, but at that moment there was no place I'd rather be.

BLUB BLUB

HMM... THE BOOK OF THOTH IS SINKING.

WE'D BETTER FISH IT OUT.

MMM-HMMPFH!

IS THERE ANYTHING ABOUT THE SERPENT'S SHADOW?

YES, HERE IT IS. IT LIES IN THE LAND OF DEMONS. SO WE'RE IN THE RIGHT PLACE. BUT THIS MAP?

THE LAND OF DEMONS IS *HUGE*. FROM WHAT I'VE READ, IT'S CONSTANTLY SHIFTING, BREAKING APART, AND RE-FORMING.

AND IT'S FULL OF DEMONS.

WE WON'T BE ABLE TO GO ANYWHERE UNSEEN, AND EVERYTHING THAT MEETS US WILL WANT TO KILL US.

I'M GUESSING *YOU* CAN GUIDE US TO THE SHADOW.

MM-MM!

HOLY HORUS, PAL! WHY DID YOU TIE ME UP?

THAT DEMON CAPTAIN WAS GOING TO TURN ON YOU ANYWAY.

THIS IS HIS *HOMELAND*! DEMONS DON'T EVER BRING MORTALS HERE UNLESS THEY'RE FOR SNACKS.

REALLY???

AND THAT'S WHY YOU WERE RUNNING AWAY WITH THE BOOK OF THOTH?

I WAS GOING TO SCOUT AHEAD!

I WANTED TO FIND THE SHADOW SO I COULD LEAD YOU THERE! BUT THAT'S NOT IMPORTANT--IF YOU LET ME GO, WE CAN FIND IT TOGETHER.

I HAVE PICKED UP SOME TRICKS THAT *ONLY GHOSTS* CAN DO.

I CAN GET YOU THERE *UNSEEN*.

UNTIE ME AND I'LL SHOW YOU.

YOU WON'T REGRET IT.

How to describe the Land of Demons?
Let's see. It was a land. It was full of demons.

The landscape was like an optical ilusion,
crumbling, rearranging itself constantlly.

Every once in a while,
Setne checked the
Book of Thoth
for directions.

THOTH DID AN
EXCELLENT JOB ON
THIS BOOK! IT SERVES
AS A MAP, COMPASS,
TOURIST'S GUIDE, AND
FARMER'S ALMANAC
TIMETABLE.

As we stumbled along, I became
more aware of the presence of Chaos.

Everything was being
pulled in the direction
we were traveling.

Exposure to
Chaos energy had
very nearly killed
me and Sadie
before, but for
some reason I
felt almost fine.

Something was protecting us, an invisible
layer of warmth keeping the Chaos at bay.

The area around Zia shimmered like vapor off a hot road.

IT IS *HER*, CARTER. RA SUSTAINS US.

Soon I heard a roar in the distance. The horizon glowed red. We seemed to be moving faster, as if we'd stepped on an automated walkway.

CAN YOU *FEEL* IT? JUST OVER THE CREST OF THIS HILL...

BEHOLD!

OUR DESTINATION!

THERE YOU GO, THE *SEA OF CHAOS*.

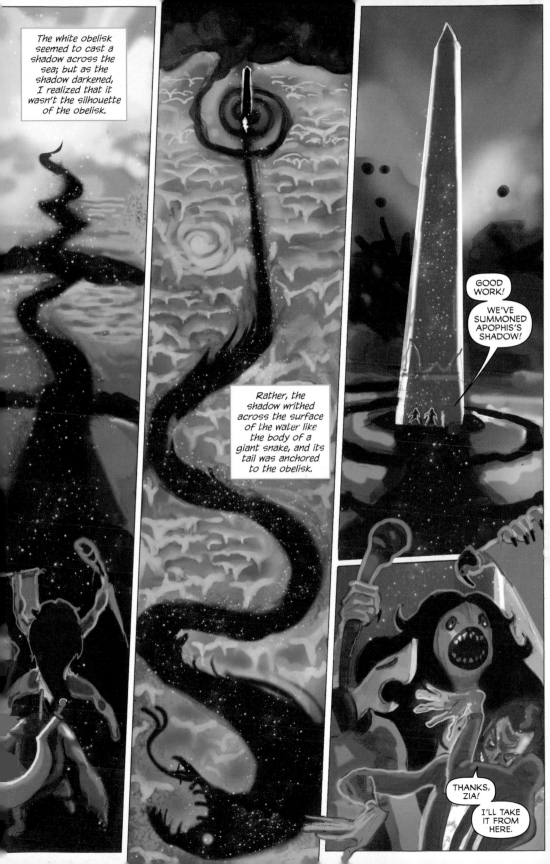

Our demon glamors suddenly turned into solid bands of mummy linen.

OH, CARTER. YOU ARE **WAY** TOO TRUSTING. AFTER THAT BUSINESS ON THE RIVERBOAT, YOU GAVE ME PERMISSION TO CAST A GLAMOR SPELL ON YOU?

CHANGING A GLAMOR INTO A STRAITJACKET IS **SOOO** EASY.

MMM!

IT'S NOTHING PERSONAL. I **NEEDED** YOU TWO! WELL-- **ONE OF YOU,** ANYWAY.

THAT **INVOCATION SPELL** HAD TO BE CAST BY A MORTAL--OR I WOULD HAVE CAST IT MYSELF AGES AGO.

APOPHIS WILL WANT TO KILL RA AND THE REST OF THE GODS, AND DESTROY THE HOUSE OF LIFE. THAT MUCH I'M FINE WITH.

BUT THE WHOLE MORTAL WORLD? NO WORRIES. I'LL SPARE MOST OF IT. I'VE GOTTA HAVE SOMEPLACE TO RULE, DON'T I?

INSTEAD OF CASTING THE EXECRATION, I'LL BLACKMAIL APOPHIS, SEE? HE'LL DESTROY ONLY WHAT I **LET** HIM DESTROY.

YEAH, YEAH. THIS IS THE PART WHERE YOU SAY, "YOU'RE MAD, SETNE! YOU'LL NEVER GET AWAY WITH IT!" BUT THE THING IS, I **WILL**.

THAT'S ANOTHER THING THIS MAGGOT LIED ABOUT. WHAT SHOULD WE DO WITH HIM? SHOVE HIM INTO THE DRINK?

MMM!

I WISH. BUT RESTRAINING OURSELVES FROM ACTS OF VENGEANCE IS WHAT MAKES US DIFFERENT FROM APOPHIS.

RULES HAVE THEIR PLACE. THEY KEEP US FROM UNRAVELING.

OSIRIS HAS TO BE THE ONE TO DECIDE SETNE'S PUNISHMENT, SINCE WE PROMISED TO BRING HIM BACK TO THE HALL OF JUDGMENT.

FINE. YOU DRAG HIM ALONG, THEN.

HE'S A GHOST. HE CAN'T BE THAT HEAVY.

Moving away from the Sea of Chaos was even harder than moving toward it.

UH-OH.

Four winged demons descended upon us.

HEH! NO DEMONS CAN WITHSTAND A *BOO BLAST*.

THE SHADOW SPELL WORKED, YOU CRAZY KID!

THANK YOU FOR GIVING ME MY LIFE BACK, AND I DON'T JUST MEAN MY SHADOW.

OKAY, GET IN THE CAR! WE'RE GOING FOR A *RIDE*.

THE GODS OF THE HOUSE OF REST ARE GOING TO COVER OUR RETREAT WHILE I GET YOU TO THE RIVER OF NIGHT.

THIS IS THE MOST FUN THEY'VE HAD IN EONS!

We played a game of hit-the-demon on our escape from the battlefield.

ONE POINT FOR THE RED DEMON!

WHACK

TWO POINTS FOR THE DRAGONFLY HEAD!

WHACK

WIPER

HEH, HEH!

The limo leaped a flaming chasm...

...and slammed to a stop on the beach of bones.

Light blazed in the darkness upriver.

HEY NOW, WE'RE JUST IN TIME TO CATCH RA'S SUN BOAT.

The crocodile-headed god **Sobek** steered from the bow, knocking aside random river monsters with a big pole.

WHEEEEEEE!

Bast was there, and sitting upon his throne, our senile friend **Ra**.

HALLOOOOOO! WE HAVE COOOOOOKIES!

CHAPTER 8

Nobody down below
was assembling.
Nobody was rejoicing.

Directly ahead, three pyramids
rose on the plains of Giza.
Sandstorms and lightning raged.

The storms took the form
of an enormous serpent.
Apophis was becoming tangible.
The desert boiled and the pyramids
shook with a horrible resonance.

Some of the oldest structures in
human history were about to crumble.

CARTER
AND SADIE KANE,
THIS IS WHERE GODS
AND MORTALS
MUST PART.

NO WAY!
WE'VE GOT THE
SHADOW. WE'RE
IN THIS FIGHT
TOGETHER!

Underground, we faced mayhem. A dozen rebels had formed a wedge blocking the doors to the **Hall of Ages**, and our initiates were trying to get past them.

It seemed backward. Shouldn't our side have been defending the doors?

We leaped into the fray, aided by the strength of Isis and Horus.

BANANA SLUG!

HAMSTER!

Walt had arrived, and he was using magic.

He tore through the enemy line, compressing rebel magicians into oversized canopic jars--while throwing other ones with inhuman strength.

He touched another rebel and instantly encased the man in mummy linen.

THWAK!

AAGH!

IS EVERYONE ALL RIGHT?

WALT, YOU'RE CURED!

AND USING MAGIC... HOW?!

Lowering my vision into the Duat revealed the truth.

"Anubis thinks there's a way to extend my life," Walt had hinted on the way back from Thoth's.

KISS
MOOCH LICK

Walt +
Anubis.
Walnubis?

OPEN THE DOORS, YOU ANNOYING BOY!

WE HAVE TO RESCUE AMOS.

Walt smiled and put his hand on the doors. Gray ash spread across the surface.

The bronze crumbled to dust and we poured into the Hall of Ages.

We didn't get far before our rescue attempt sputtered to a stop.

Hovering midair in the center of the hall was the strangest *avatar* I'd ever seen. Part sandstorm, part fire, vaguely human.

The good news: Amos wasn't fighting alone. The bad news: his backup was the god of Chaos.

THIS IS FUN, LITTLE MAGICIANS! DON'T YOU HAVE ANY MORE TRICKS?

SET! NO KILLING!

It was hard to comprehend that Amos would ever **willingly** channel the red god's power.

Yet he was doing the impossible.

He was **winning**.

BAH! COME ON, AMOS, LET ME HAVE SOME FUN.

I. ONLY WANT TO STRIP THE FLESH FROM THEIR BONES!

To say Apophis was huge would be like saying **the Titanic** took on a little water.

Since we'd been underground, the serpent had grown. Now his coils stretched across the desert for miles, wrapping around the pyramids and tunneling under the outskirts of Cairo, lifting entire neighborhoods like old carpeting.

He dashed Ra's sun boat into kindling with one flick of his tongue.

منوع التسلق
No Climbing

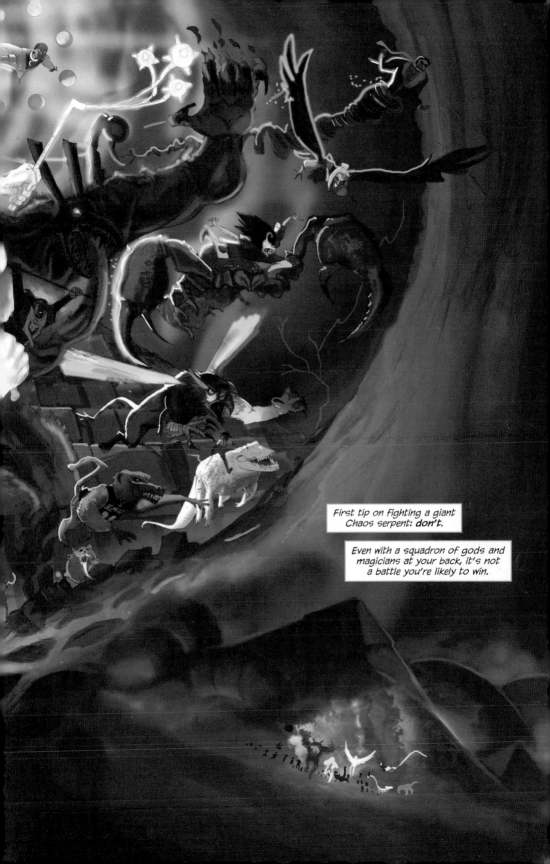

First tip on fighting a giant Chaos serpent: **don't**.

Even with a squadron of gods and magicians at your back, it's not a battle you're likely to win.

As we charged closer, the world fractured. Apophis slithered in and out of the desert as well as in and out of the Duat, splintering reality into different layers.

Hapi rode one version of the serpent's head, his massive fists pounding between Apophis's eyes.

Neith sniped at another snakehead with her arrows.

Amos and Set sliced through the empty air, shouting command words at nothing.

The goddess Serqet rode a giant black scorpion parrying a version of Apophis's tail with her stinger in a bizarre sword fight.

Our allies fell aside in Apophis's fun house of evil. Ra's crook and flail guided Carter toward the sun god. Apophis's sheut guided me toward the serpent.

It felt like we were running through layers of clear syrup, each thicker and more resistant than the next.

WE HAVE TO GET TO RA. CONCENTRATE ON HIM!

Ahead of us, a bright light shimmered as if through fifty feet of water.

He was cut short (literally) when his head exploded.

Yes, it was just as gross as it sounds.

The body of Apophis crumbled into sand and steaming goo.

EPILOGUE

Amos called a general assembly in the Hall of Ages, so we made our way back underground.

The mood in the First Nome was light and festive.

Magicians were trading stories, mingling and checking in with old friends.

PSSSST!

YOU DID GOOD, PAL. NOT THE WAY I WOULD'VE HANDLED IT, BUT NOT BAD.

TAS!

OH, NOT THAT. WE'RE DONE PLAYING THAT GAME.

BUT DON'T WORRY, PAL. I'LL SEE YOU AROUND.

I SUPPOSE WE'LL HAVE TO DEAL WITH THAT GIT SOONER OR LATER, BUT FOR NOW LET'S GO TO THE GENERAL ASSEMBLY.

CARTER AND SADIE, ON BEHALF OF THE HOUSE OF LIFE, I THANK YOU. YOU HAVE RESTORED MA'AT!

APOPHIS HAS BEEN EXECRATED, AND RA HAS ONCE AGAIN RISEN INTO THE HEAVENS, BUT THIS TIME IN TRIUMPH.

WELL DONE!

The crowd applauded wildly. Either they approved of me, or they were relieved that a kid wasn't going to be giving them daily orders from the throne.

The best part of saving the world? The after-party, of course!

For the first night in ages, we'd be able to sleep easy.

The next morning, we packed up for a morning flight back to Brooklyn.

Carter stayed behind.

I wanted some more time with Zia. A proper date.

The same tunnel system that connected the First Nome with Giza also happened to be tied to the Cairo metro in the downtown center.

UM, AFTER YOU, ZIA!

AMOS HAS LOTS OF HELP AT THE FIRST NOME NOW. HE THOUGHT IT WOULD BE GOOD FOR ME TO SPEND SOME TIME AWAY, TRY TO LIVE A MORE TYPICAL LIFE.

YOU MEAN, LIKE, LEAVE EGYPT?

YOUR SISTER SUGGESTED I STAY AT BROOKLYN HOUSE AND ATTEND AMERICAN SCHOOL. SHE SAID--HOW DID SHE PUT IT...?

"AMERICANS ARE AN ODD BUNCH, BUT THEY GROW ON YOU."

WOULD YOU MIND IF I STAYED IN BROOKLYN HOUSE? I COULD HELP TEACH THE INITIATES. BUT IF THAT WOULD MAKE YOU UNCOMFORTABLE--

NO! I MEAN, NO, I DON'T MIND. YES, I'D LIKE THAT. A LOT. QUITE A BIT. TOTALLY FINE.

SO THAT'S A YES?

YES. I MEAN, UNLESS IT WOULD MAKE YOU UNCOMFORTABLE.

I WOULDN'T WANT TO MAKE THINGS AWKWARD OR--

CARTER?

HUSH.

Back in Brooklyn, a familiar figure waited for me at Freak's roost.

WALT?! WHAT ARE YOU WEARING?

ANUBIS PICKED IT. NOW THAT OUR BODIES ARE MERGED, WE HAVE TO SHARE STYLES TOO.

IS THIS ANOTHER GOOD-BYE? I'VE HAD ENOUGH GOOD-BYES TODAY.

ACTUALLY, IT'S MORE OF A HELLO. MY NAME'S WALT STONE, FROM SEATTLE. I'D LIKE TO JOIN THE PARTY.

He was repeating exactly what he'd said the day he arrived at Brooklyn House.

VERY FUNNY. YOU THINK YOU CAN JUST MERGE WITH A GOD AND SURPRISE ME WITH AN "OH, BY THE WAY, I'M ACTUALLY TWO MINDS IN ONE BODY"?

I DON'T APPRECIATE BEING TAKEN OFF GUARD.

I DID TRY TO TELL YOU, SEVERAL TIMES. ANUBIS DID TOO. WE KEPT GETTING INTERRUPTED.

NO EXCUSE.

I'M STILL WALT. ANUBIS CAN STAY IN THIS WORLD AS LONG AS I'M HIS HOST, AND I'M HOPING TO LIVE A GOOD LONG LIFE.

I'M NOT GOING ANYWHERE, UNLESS YOU WANT ME TO LEAVE.

My eyes probably answered for me: No, please. Not ever.

But I couldn't very well give him the satisfaction of my saying that out loud, could I?

WELL, I SUPPOSE I COULD TOLERATE IT.

I OWE YOU A DANCE. MAY I?

HERE? WON'T YOUR CHAPERONE SHU INTERRUPT?

I'M *MORTAL* NOW. HE'LL LET US DANCE, THOUGH I'M SURE HE'S KEEPING AN EYE ON US TO MAKE SURE WE BEHAVE.

TO MAKE SURE *YOU* BEHAVE.

I'M A PROPER YOUNG LADY.

I'LL HAVE YOU REMEMBER THAT MY FATHER IS YOUR EMPLOYER IN THE UNDERWORLD. YOU'D BEST MIND YOUR MANNERS.

YES, MA'AM.

SO YOU'LL LET ME STICK AROUND? LET ME EXPERIENCE A TYPICAL TEENAGE LIFE?

I SUPPOSE. NOT THAT I'M AN EXPERT MYSELF, BUT THERE IS ONE RULE I INSIST ON.

IF ANYONE ASKS YOU IF YOU'RE TAKEN, THE ANSWER IS YES.

GOOD, BECAUSE YOU DON'T WANT TO SEE ME *CROSS*.

TOO LATE.

I THINK I CAN LIVE WITH THAT.

SHUT UP AND DANCE, WALT.

As for you lot out there, we're never too busy for new initiates. If you have the blood of the pharaohs, what are you waiting for? Don't let your magic go to waste.

Brooklyn House is open for business!

PUFFIN BOOKS

UK | USA | Canada | Ireland | Australia
India | New Zealand | South Africa

Puffin Books is part of the Penguin Random House group of companies
whose addresses can be found at global.penguinrandomhouse.com.

www.penguin.co.uk
www.puffin.co.uk
www.ladybird.co.uk

Penguin
Random House
UK

Adapted from the novel *The Kane Chronicles: The Serpent's Shadow*
published in Great Britain by Puffin Books

Graphic novel first published in USA by Disney•Hyperion Books,
an imprint of Disney Book Group, 2017
Published simultaneously in Great Britain by Puffin Books 2017
001

A CIP catalogue record for this book is available from the British Library

Printed in China

ISBN: 978–0–241–33680–9

MIX
Paper from
responsible sources
FSC® C018179

Penguin Random House is committed to a
sustainable future for our business, our readers
and our planet. This book is made from Forest
Stewardship Council® certified paper.